Parents and Caregivers,

Stone Arch Readers are designed to provid[e] experiences, as well as opportunities to de[velop] literacy skills, and comprehension. Here are a few ways to support your beginning reader:

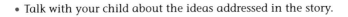

- Talk with your child about the ideas addressed in the story.

- Discuss each illustration, mentioning the characters, where they are, and what they are doing.

- Read with expression, pointing to each word. You may want to read the whole story through and then revisit parts of the story to ensure that the meanings of words or phrases are understood.

- Talk about why the character did what he or she did and what your child would do in that situation.

- Help your child connect with characters and events in the story.

Remember, reading with your child should be fun, not forced. Each moment spent reading with your child is a priceless investment in his or her literacy life.

Gail Saunders-Smith, Ph.D.

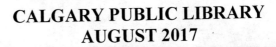

STONE ARCH READERS

are published by Stone Arch Books, a Capstone Imprint
1710 Roe Crest Drive
North Mankato, Minnesota 56003
www.capstonepub.com

Library of Congress Cataloging-in-Publication data
is available on the Library of Congress website.

ISBN 978-1-4342-4016-3 (library binding)
ISBN 978-1-4342-4238-9 (paperback)

Reading Consultants:
Gail Saunders-Smith, Ph.D.
Melinda Melton Crow, M.Ed.
Laurie K. Holland, Media Specialist

Designer: Hilary Wacholz

Printed in China
032012   006677RRDF12

Let's Paint the Garage!

written by
Melinda Melton Crow

illustrated by
Chad Thompson

STONE ARCH BOOKS
a capstone imprint

School Bus, Tractor, Fire Truck, and Train were friends.

They lived in a big garage.

The garage was old.

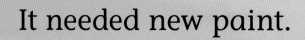

It needed new paint.

Tractor painted his stall green.

"My home looks great!"
said Tractor.

School Bus painted his
stall yellow.

"My home looks great!"
said School Bus.

Train painted his stall blue.

"My home looks great!"
said Train.

Fire Truck painted his stall red.

25

"My home looks great, too!"
said Fire Truck.

The garage needed one
more thing.

New signs! Now the garage was done.

STORY WORDS

friends   painted   stall

garage   color   home

Total Word Count: 86